Pirate Stories
for Little Boys

Pirate Stories
for Little Boys

Russell Punter

Illustrated by Benji Davies,
Christyan Fox and Kate Sheppard

Contents

Pirates Ahoy!

"Wait for me!" yelled Ben Buckle. He was cabin boy aboard *The Jolly Rascal.*

8

And his ship
was about to set
sail on a hunt for
treasure.

As the ship left port, Ben took
Captain Cutlass his sea charts.

Thankee, boy!

The ship sailed
all day and into
the starry night.

Ben felt the sea getting rougher and rougher.

Suddenly, they were
in the middle of a
massive storm.

The ship lurched from side to side.

Huge waves crashed onto the deck.

Ben clung to the mast in panic. "I hope we don't capsize!" he thought.

At last, the storm blew itself out, and the pirates started patching up the sails.

This will take some mending!

14

Ben watched as Captain Cutlass and the crew leaped aboard the other ship.

Swords clanged.

Sailors yelped.

Pirates yelled.

Take 'em alive, lads!

Yikes!

Help!

The ship's crew was
put into a boat...

and brought aboard
The Jolly Rascal.

"Don't worry," said Captain Cutlass.
"We'll put you ashore at the next island."

Caw!
Welcome aboard!

After dropping off the sailors, the pirates had a party.
The ship shook with sea shanties and jolly jigs, until...

Ben and the others scrambled on deck.

Soon *The Jolly Rascal* was racing through the water.

Full speed ahead, lads!

They hid in a sheltered cove as the pirate hunters sailed past.

"We escaped!" gasped Ben in relief.

"On to our next adventure!" cried Captain Cutlass.

26

The Pesky Parrot

Charlie Crossbones had just left Pirate School.

He knew how to read a map...

Ah!

unlock a treasure chest...

Click!

raise **The Jolly Roger**...

and do a proper pirate's laugh.

Ha..har..har!

He had all he needed to be a pirate.

Except for one thing...

He didn't have a parrot!

And then, down by the docks, Charlie found parrots galore.

USED PARROT SALE

Get the bird here!

Parrots going cheap!

To his dismay, the parrots were all
far too expensive.

Then the parrot seller took pity on him.

"There is one bird you could have," he said.

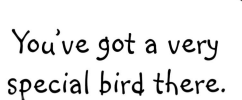

You've got a very special bird there.

Charlie had never seen such a pretty parrot – and it only cost a penny.

Now Charlie and his parrot could sail the Seven Seas in search of treasure.

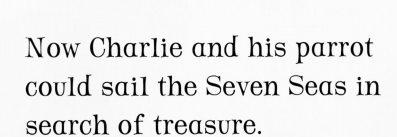

Out at sea, Charlie soon spotted a ship he recognized –
The Fat Flounder, belonging to Captain Silverside.

Charlie slipped into his rowing boat. Quickly and quietly, he rowed over to the ship.

Then he sneaked in through an open window.

He was in luck. He'd found the captain's treasure cabin.

But, as he stuffed his pockets with jewels, disaster struck!

"Sssh!" Charlie hissed at his parrot.
It was too late.

Captain Silverside and his crew chased Charlie around the deck six times.

Come back, you sneaky thief!

Puffing and panting, Charlie only just escaped to his boat.

Charlie turned to his parrot with a face like thunder.

Don't ever do that again, you pesky parrot!

But every time they went to sea, the parrot caused trouble.

Just as Charlie was about to steal
someone's treasure...

...the parrot let out a warning screech.

Charlie had had enough.

He tried to get rid of
the parrot...

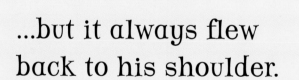

...but it always flew
back to his shoulder.

So Charlie went to the local inn for dinner, to cheer himself up.

The Laughing Lobster Inn
Super Deluxe Menu
Scrummy Scampi 7 pennies
Mouthwatering Mussels 6 pennies
Deluxe Menu
Crispy Cod 5 pennies
Fancy Fishcakes 4 pennies
Cheap Menu
Shrimp on toast 3 pennies
Very Cheap Menu
Bread and cheese 1 penny
(free jug of water with all orders)

Thanks to that pesky parrot, he only had enough money for bread and cheese.

While Charlie was talking to
Mr. Grog, the innkeeper...

...a thief was creeping up
to Mr. Grog's cash box.

The crook was about to strike, when Charlie's parrot squawked into action.

Stop thief!

"What a wonderful bird!" said Mr. Grog.

"That thief nearly got away with my cash."

This gave Charlie an idea.
He sold his parrot to the innkeeper.

Mr. Grog was delighted with his new burglar alarm...

Stop thief!

the parrot enjoyed his new job...

...and Charlie bought another bird – a quiet one this time!

Captain Spike

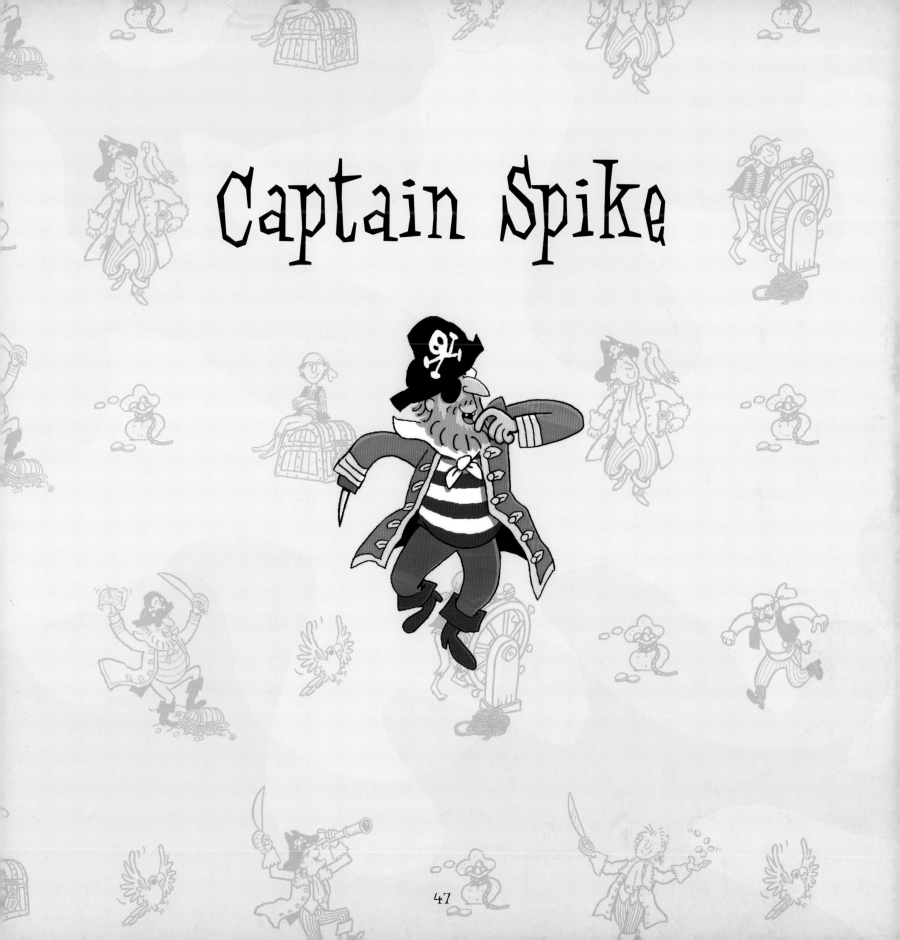

Macintosh Mullet was a poor, poor fisherman.

He lived on tiny Mullet Island with his only daughter, Molly.

One morning, Macintosh gave a sad sigh.

He hadn't caught any fish for a month.

Molly packed their valuables into
a chest and left for the mainland.

Less than ten minutes later, Molly was grabbed by Captain Spike and his band of pirates.

Spike tried everything to find out
where Molly had hidden the
key to the chest.

He tickled her.

Yuck!

He fed her stale ship's
biscuits.

Molly refused
to talk.

Spike was losing patience, when a thick fog
swirled around the ship.

"Help! Where are we? We can't see," wailed the pirates.

"I know these waters," said Molly. "I'll guide you home... if you let me go afterwards."

After an hour, the fog began to clear.

"I'll take over from here," boomed Spike.
"YOU can walk the plank!"

Spike made Molly walk off a plank...

into the shark-filled sea.

But, instead of a **splash**, all the pirates heard was a thud!

At that moment, the last of the fog lifted.

"This isn't Shark Island!" growled Spike.

"We've been tricked!"

Molly had steered them into port.

The port police carried off the pirates to jail.

And clever Molly carried off a big reward.

Percy and the Pirates

Percy Pike lived with his family by the sea.

Most of the time he was happy.

But not at meal times.

There was never enough to eat.

Percy's tummy often rumbled all day long.

So Percy made a plan.

He borrowed his dad's boat and rowed out to sea.

Dangling his fishing rod over the side,
he waited for the fish to bite...

But all he got was a leak...

in the bottom of his boat.

Luckily, he was rescued by a passing ship.

Unluckily, it was a passing pirate ship.

"I'm Captain Crook and this is my crew!" bellowed a red-faced man.

My name's Percy Pike.

"Tell Percy what we do on this ship, lads,"
Captain Crook barked.

The three crew members burst into song...

We steal for Crook, 'cos he's the best,
Then put the treasure in his chest.

"Or else you'll walk the plank," said Crook.

Percy didn't want to be a pirate...

but he didn't want to be shark food either.

"Ship ahoy!" shouted a pirate.

"Board her, boys!" ordered
Captain Crook.

The three pirates swung
across to the other ship...

chased her crew
around the deck...

and came back with bags
bursting with gold, silver
and diamonds.

The pirates poured the treasure into
Captain Crook's chest.

Well, almost all the treasure...

That night, Crook found gold
in Sam Scurvy's locker...

diamonds under Willy
Weevil's bunk...

...and silver in Ronnie
Rum's spare sea boots.

"No one steals from me!" growled Captain Crook.

The double-crossing crew were forced to walk the plank.

Percy was the only one left.

"We're going on a night raid," said Crook.

"And no tricks when we get on that ship," he warned.

While the crew of the ship snored in their bunks,
Percy searched the cabins.

Instead of treasure, he only found maps –
but they gave him a brilliant idea.

He grabbed a quill, and picked out a map of a nearby island.

First, he drew a wiggly arrow across the island...

Then he added an 'X' at the end of the arrow...

Last of all, he wrote 'treasure' underneath the 'X'.

Percy crept out to Captain Crook with the map.
"I found a treasure map," he whispered.

"Ha!" said Crook, snatching it.

"Soon I'll be rich!" he crowed,
as they rowed back to his ship.

At dawn, they reached the island on the map.

They followed
Percy's arrow, past
palm trees...

between
spiky rocks...

around a
lake...

and over a
rushing river...

until they
reached
the 'X'.

"Give me that shovel, boy!" yelled the captain.

Crook began digging furiously.

Soon he was **deep, deep** down underground.

"Just you wait until I get out of here!"
Captain Crook screamed at Percy.

But however hard he tried...

he couldn't
climb out.

Percy took his chance.

"Cheerio, Captain!" he shouted, and
he ran back to the pirate ship.

Percy lowered the Jolly Roger and set sail.
In no time he was cruising into his home port.

Percy returned Crook's booty to its owners.

They were so grateful, they gave him his very own bulging treasure chest as a reward.

Percy arrived home a hero.

And the Pike family never went hungry again.

The Masked Pirate

WANTED

The Masked Pirate

BIG REWARD!

S
am Sardine dreamed of becoming a sailor.

He wanted to explore the Seven Seas, and do battle with bloodthirsty pirates.

So he joined Captain Winkle's crew.

But life on board ship wasn't as thrilling
as Sam had hoped.

He spent all day
mopping the decks...

peeling potatoes...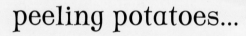

and washing the sailors'
smelly socks.

After a month, Sam asked the captain
for a more exciting job.

"All right then," said Captain Winkle.
"Let's see you sail the ship into port."

Sam's chest swelled with pride as he took the wheel.

But steering a ship wasn't as easy as it looked...

"Um, maybe I should start with
something simpler," said Sam.

Captain Winkle agreed.

He told Sam to guard the ship's treasure while the crew slept.

But Sam was so tired after sailing the ship, that he drifted...

off...

to...

sleep.

The next morning, Sam was woken by a wicked laugh.

The dreaded Masked Pirate had sneaked in and stolen the captain's treasure!

When the captain heard, he was not too happy.

After he'd calmed down, he offered a reward to whoever found the thief or his treasure.

But no one knew what the Masked Pirate looked like without his disguise.

Then Sam smiled. He'd had an idea.

He left at once to spend the night at The Spyglass Inn, which was always full of pirates.

The next morning over breakfast,
Sam announced,

"I heard the Masked Pirate talking
in his sleep last night."

He described the spot
where he hides his
treasure.

One particular pirate frowned at Sam.

Sam's plan was working.

"Now I know where the treasure is, I'll get it for myself," said Sam.

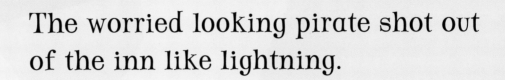

The worried looking pirate shot out of the inn like lightning.

Sam followed close behind.

The pirate jumped into a boat and rowed as fast as he could to a nearby island.

Sam raced to Captain Winkle.

"Follow that pirate!" he cried.

On the island, the pirate
was heaving a treasure
chest out of the sand.

Captain Winkle recognized it at once. It was his chest!

"Take my ship and get help, Sam!" he shouted.

The reward money is yours, Sam!

"You trust me to sail?" said Sam, with a sharp salute. That was the best reward of all.

Pirate of the Year

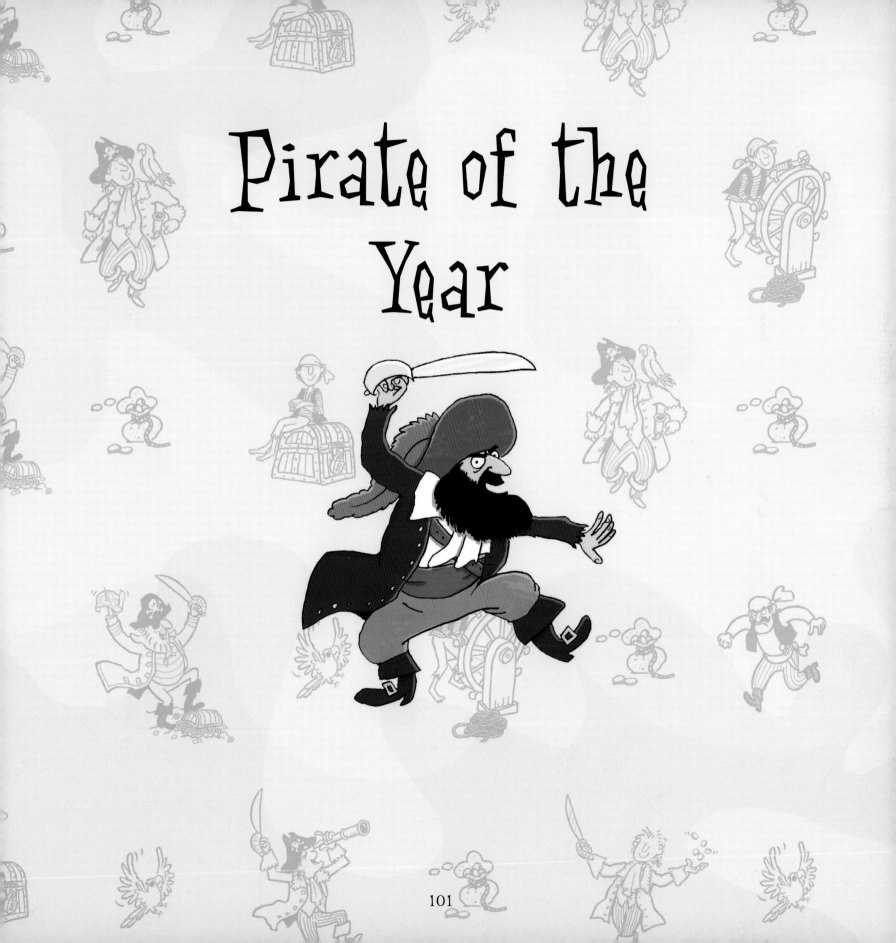

Today was the final of the
Pirate of the Year contest.

There were only two contestants left –
Captain Blackheart and Billy Booty.

The lucky winner would receive a chest full of treasure.

Ye scoreboard

Blackheart   Billy

Rules

1. Cheating is expected. (Just don't get caught.)

2. Pirates <u>must</u> protect each other against danger.

Task one was a flat-out galleon race to Skull Island and back.

Ear-splitting cannon fire started them off.

Billy quickly took the lead.

But as soon as the ships were out of sight of
the judges, Blackheart got to work.

Flaps opened in his ship's hull,
and ten oars shot out.

"All right, lads," he cried to his crew.
"Start rowing!"

"Cheat!" yelled Billy, as Blackheart raced by.

"Remember rule one!" laughed Blackheart.

When the judges came in sight,
Blackheart's crew whipped in their oars.

"I win!" cried Blackheart, crossing the finish line with a whoop.

Blackheart	Billy
1	0

Next, they had to dive for a silver chest.

Blackheart gave Billy a big hug. "Good luck, matey!" he boomed.

The pirates plunged into the water and

dived down, down, down...

to the seabed.

Billy grabbed the chest and was heading back when...

...three sharks appeared from nowhere and surrounded him, grinning fiercely.

Billy dropped the chest and swam for his life.

Seconds later, Blackheart surfaced triumphantly, clutching the chest himself.

Billy felt something slimy in his swimsuit pocket.
"So that's why Blackheart hugged me," he thought.

He knew the sharks would come after this.

Parrot training was next. The pirate with the chattiest bird would triumph.

Billy's parrot, Mimi, went first.

Pieces of eight!

Ship ahoy!

Pretty boy!

"Beat that, Blackheart!" said Billy, with a smile.

"Ha!" scoffed his opponent. "Wait until you hear my bird, Hook Beak."

"Hook Beak's the winner!" declared a judge.

Only Blackheart knew that it was one of his crew who'd really done the talking.

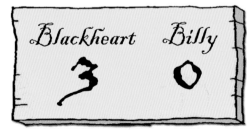

With Blackheart in the lead, it was time for the final task.

On the shore of Skull Island,
each pirate was given a map.

The first one to find their buried
treasure chest would win.

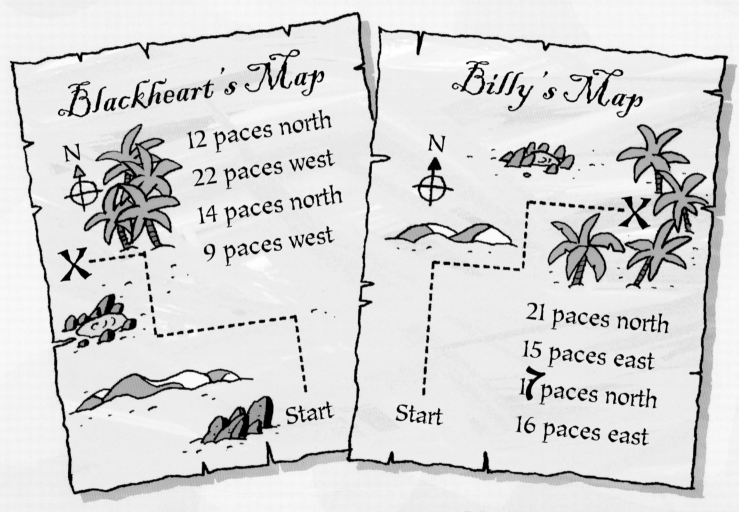

Blackheart's Map

N

12 paces north
22 paces west
14 paces north
9 paces west

X

Start

Billy's Map

N

X

21 paces north
15 paces east
17 paces north
16 paces east

Start

There was something odd about Billy's map
– but he had no time to hesitate.

The pirates paced out their routes.

But Billy forgot to look where he was going.

He walked straight into a rock pool full of angry crabs.

"Blackheart added six extra paces to my map," thought Billy, as crazy crabs pinched him all over.

Meanwhile, Blackheart had found the chest and bounded across the beach to show the judges.

"I win... aaagh!" he yelped. "Help me! Quick!
I'm sinking in quicksand."

Billy snapped a branch from a
palm tree. "Grab this!" he called.

Hauling and heaving, he
dragged his rival to safety.

"Well done, Billy!" cheered the crowd.

"I still won the task," sniffed the ungrateful Blackheart.

"One point for Blackheart," agreed the judges.
"But five bonus points to Billy for saving his life."

"Pirate of the Year!" squawked
Mimi proudly, as Billy was
given the prize.

Blackheart   Billy

4   5

118

The Return of Captain Spike

On the shore of Rotter's Isle stood a gloomy old castle.

But this was no ordinary castle.
It was a prison – for pirates!

Once a month, a ship full of prisoners arrived.

HMS Con Carrier

The pirates were marched ashore and thrown into the dark, dank dungeons.

No one had ever escaped from Rotter's Isle.

The newest prisoner was
selfish Captain Spike.

He was so mean, even other pirates hated him.

From the day Spike arrived,
things went missing.

Cut-throat Craig's pocket
watch disappeared.

Roger Redbeard's silver
earring vanished in the night.

And Sidney Skull
lost his gold locket.

No one knew who the thief was.

But Bobby Bones noticed Spike's booty bag getting fuller and fuller...

When Spike wasn't sneaking around, he was busy showing off.

"No jail can hold me!" he bragged. "I'm going to escape."

"Ha!" laughed Bobby Bones.
"I bet you'll be back in twenty-four hours."

"What do you bet?" asked Spike.

"My treasure map," replied Bobby.
"Stay out for more than a day, and
I'll send it to you."

"You're on!" agreed Spike.

"Address it to The Spyglass Inn," said Spike confidently. "It'll reach me there."

"But if you fail," said Bobby,
"I get everything in your booty bag."

Spike couldn't wait to get his hands on the map.

That night, he took it from under Billy's pillow.

He unlocked the cell door with a stolen key.

Then he crept past the guards and
down to the dock.

Stealing a small boat, he set sail.

Using the stars to guide him, Spike followed the
directions on Billy's treasure map.

As it got light, Spike saw land.

"That must be the island on the map," he thought.

Once ashore, he followed the directions to the treasure...

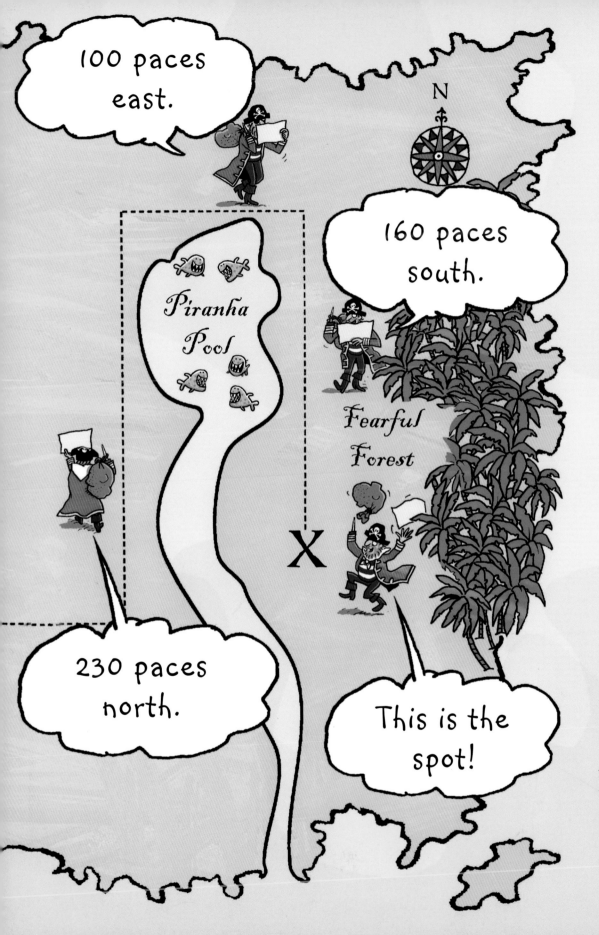

"Yippee! I'll soon be rich!" he yelled.

Spike took a shovel from his bag
and began digging.

The loot can join the booty in my bag.

"Bobby Bones was a fool to tell me about his map!"
laughed the treacherous pirate.

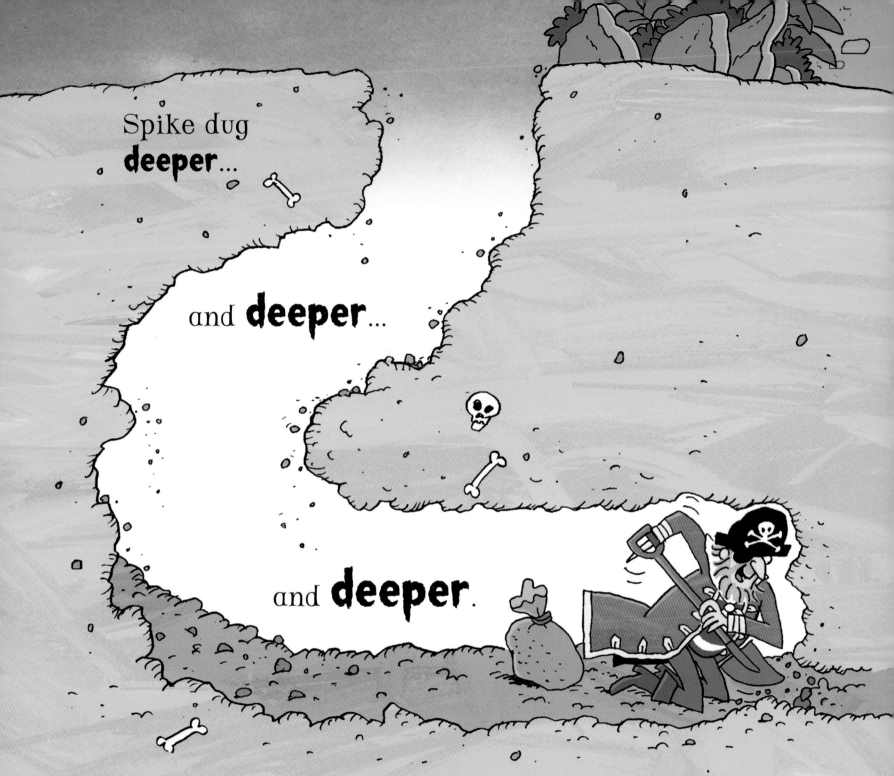

Spike dug **deeper**...

and **deeper**...

and **deeper**.

He shook with excitement as the ground moved beneath him. "This is it!" he cried.

The next moment, Spike tumbled downward
and landed bump! on a cold, stone floor.

"Welcome back!" shouted Bobby Bones.

Silly Spike had fallen for Bobby's trick.

He had sailed right around Rotter's Isle and was back where he started.

With thanks to Sarah Courtauld

Edited by Jenny Tyler and Lesley Sims

Cover design by Caroline Spatz

First published in 2010 by Usborne Publishing Ltd., Usborne House, 83-85 Saffron Hill, London EC1N 8RT, England. www.usborne.com
Copyright © 2010 Usborne Publishing Ltd.